Cow Can't Sleep

by **Ken Baker**   illustrated by **Steve Gray**

Amazon Children's Publishing

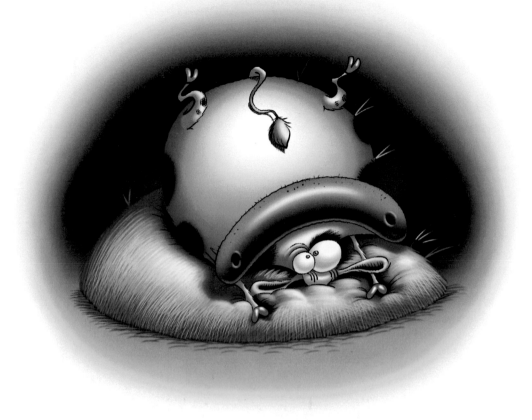

Amazon Publishing
Attn: Amazon Children's Books
P.O. Box 400818
Las Vegas, NV 89149
www.amazon.com/amazonchildrenspublishing

 **Pinwheel Books**

The illustrations are rendered in digital media.
Book design by Vera Soki
Editor: Marilyn Brigham

Printed in China (W)
10 9 8 7 6 5 4 3 2 1

Library of Congress Cataloging-in-Publication Data
Baker, Ken, 1962-
 Cow can't sleep / by Ken Baker ; illustrated by Steve Gray. — 1st
Marshall Cavendish Pinwheel Books ed.
   p. cm.
 Summary: Unable to sleep on the scratchy hay in the barn, Belle gets
the farmyard in an uproar before she finds a soft, quiet place to sleep.
 ISBN 978-0-7614-6198-2 (hardcover) — ISBN 978-0-7614-6199-9 (ebook)
[1. Cows—Fiction. 2. Sleep—Fiction. 3. Domestic animals—Fiction. 4.
Farms—Fiction.] I. Gray, Steve, 1950- ill. II. Title. III. Title: Cow cannot
sleep.
 PZ7.B17428Cow 2012   [E]—dc23   2011036606

To Mom and Dad—thanks for your wonderful love,
care, support, and example
—K. B.

To Pammy Gray—
Mom still can't get you to go to bed!
—S. G.

Belle tiptoed out of the barn. She couldn't sleep. The hay was too scratchy.

It was dark out, but Belle found
a nice feathered mattress.

But the mattress was too lumpy, too loud.

Belle still couldn't sleep. She needed a drink.
She found a big glass of water, but . . .

. . . she took too big of a slurp and fell in!

Now Belle was too cold and
too wet to sleep, until . . .

... she found some warm wool blankets to snuggle in.

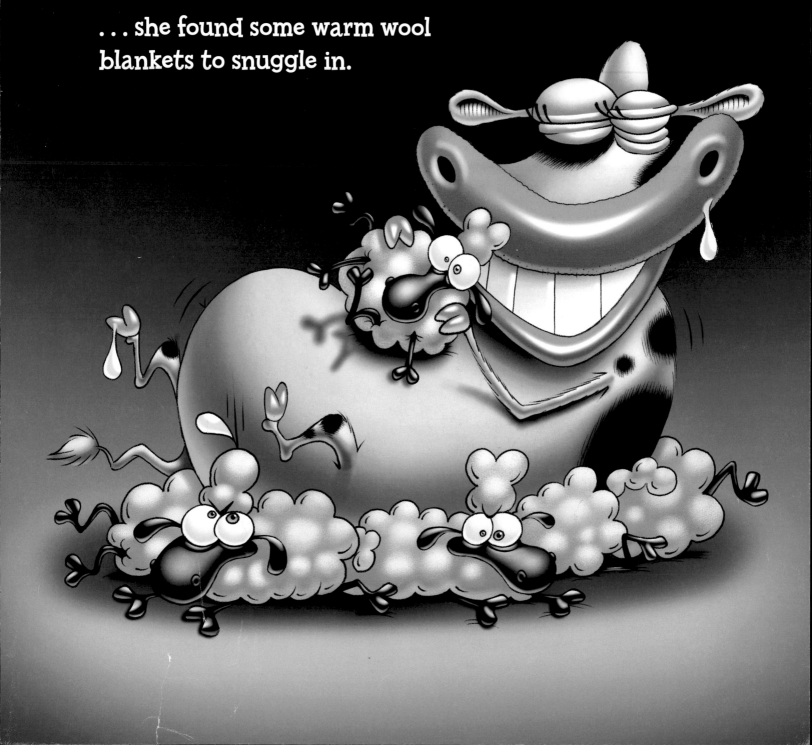

The blankets did NOT like to snuggle.
They kept moving around.

BAAAₐ!

Finally, Belle found a soft bed of mud to sleep in.
It was perfect, except . . .

. . . it started to bubble, gurgle, and really stink.
Belle plugged her nose and ran.

She tried to hide in the chicken coop,
but the stink made her sneeze. *Achoo!!*

She tried to hide in the doghouse. *Achoo!!*

When she finally stopped sneezing, Belle decided she was better off where she started—in the hay.

But it was too noisy.

So Belle found a nice
quiet place . . .

. . . with a nice soft bed,

. . . and fell right to sleep!